REGULAR SHOW

BIG
SUMMER VACATION
ACTIVITY BOOK

BY JAKE BLACK

CARTOON NETWORK BOOKS

An Imprint of Penguin Group (USA) LLC

D1530094

CARTOON NETWORK BOOKS
Published by the Penguin Group
Penguin Group (USA) LLC, 375 Hudson Street, New York, New York 10014, USA

USA | Canada | UK | Ireland | Australia | New Zealand | India | South Africa | China

penguin.com
A Penguin Random House Company

Photo credits: page 7: (drum kit) © Thinkstock, photo by Annykos; page 16: (flower pot) © Thinkstock, photo by dramaj; page 25: (dishes) © Thinkstock, photo by incomible; page 29: (compass) © Thinkstock, photo by Bercutt; page 35: (sweater) © Thinkstock, photo by kite-kit; postcards: (Mount Rushmore) © Thinkstock, photo by AndreyKrav; (Monument Valley) © Thinkstock, photo by ventdusud; (Statue of Liberty) © Thinkstock, photo by Global_Pics; (Golden Gate Bridge) © Thinkstock, photo by somchaij.

Published in 2015 by Cartoon Network Books, an imprint of Penguin Group (USA) LLC, 345 Hudson Street, New York, New York 10014. Manufactured in China.

ISBN 978-0-8431-8281-1

10 9 8 7 6 5 4 3 2

Grab a deck chair, pour a big glass of lemonade, and get ready for awesome summer activities with Mordecai, Rigby, and the rest of the gang from *Regular Show*!

Warm-Up

What's up, dudes! It's summertime, and that means it's time to parrrr-tay! This book will totally hook you up so you won't be completely bored this summer. But don't start drawing or doing the activities until you've warmed up! Check out Mordecai and Rigby below, and draw the pic on the next page!

Freeway Maze

The guys have got to pick up a ton of supplies for the Park from across town, but the freeway is really messed up with all these dead ends and crazy turns and stuff. Get them through the maze of the highway in time so they won't get fired!

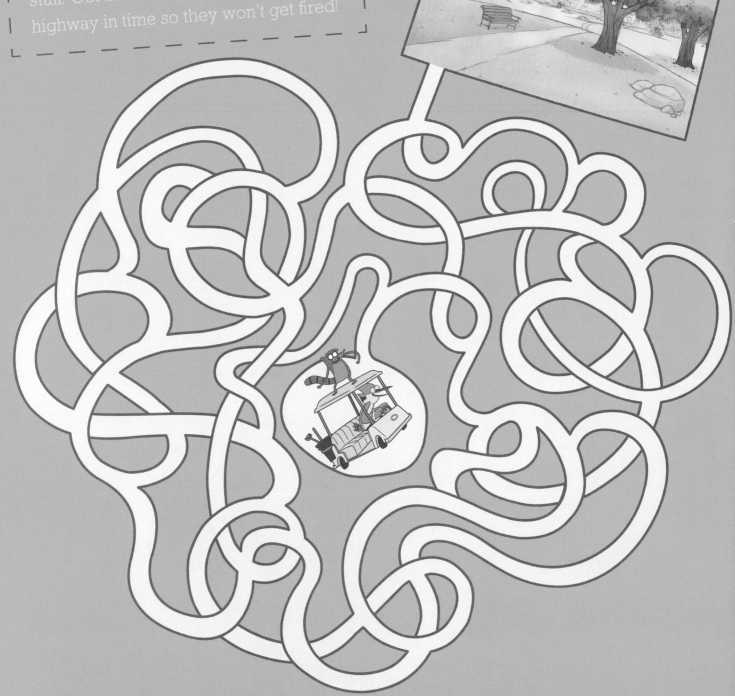

Benson's Drummin'

You might not believe this, but Benson is an awesome drummer. On his drum kit below, draw the logos of his band. Like, with skulls and fire and stuff. Or rainbows and unicorns. Whatever.

Muscle Man's Hairdo

Muscle Man develops a bald spot and doesn't want Starla to find out. Cover up the spot any way you can. Draw a hat! Plant some grass! Stick a duck on it! Starla can't see him like this!

Fitness

Time to get off the couch and get some exercise! Eileen is ready to help you finish the Park's Fitness Challenge! Write down how many of each exercise you did in the space provided next to it.

Push-ups

_____

Challenges

Sit-ups

_____

Pull-ups

_____

Jumping jacks

_____

Jogging in place

_____ minutes

Party Planner

Remember that one party Mordecai and Rigby
went to? It was amazing! It's time to plan your own!

What day is the party?

What time?

What are you going to eat?

Whom are you going to invite?

What are you going to do?
Dance? Play games?

Fireworks Show

Fireworks shows are the best part of summer! But Muscle Man accidentally set off the fireworks for the Park's big fireworks show. It's up to you to draw the fireworks for the show so no one is disappointed!

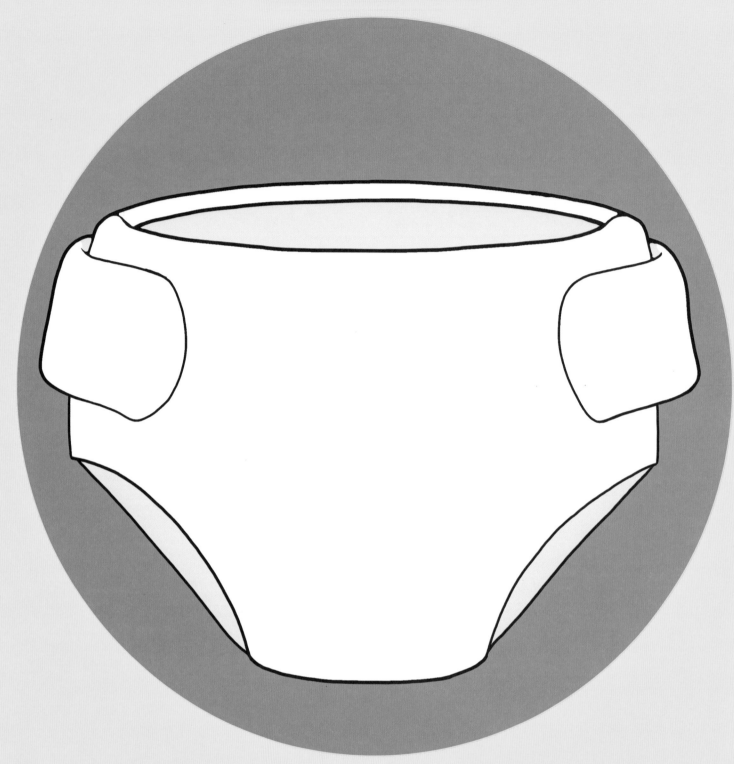

Designer Diapers

Oh man! Mordecai lost a bet and has to wear a diaper for a week! But it won't be so bad if he can have a kickin' designer diaper. Do your best diaper design so Mordecai looks awesome!

Eileen is taking care of Margaret's flowers, but she's overwatered them, so they're growing out of control. Draw a pot of flowers!

Makeup

Starla's got a big date with Muscle Man tonight, but she can't decide how she should do her makeup. Draw on any jewelry she might wear, and do her makeup for her. The brighter the lipstick, the better!

Fool Me Twice Games

The games on Fool Me Twice are crazy, dangerous, wild, and awesome! Mordecai and Rigby are the only contestants to survive the games, so they've been invited back to the show. Draw their games.

Album Cover

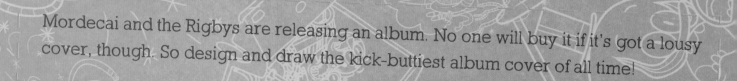

Mordecai and the Rigbys are releasing an album. No one will buy it if it's got a lousy cover, though. So design and draw the kick-buttiest album cover of all time!

START

FINISH

Airport Maze

Margaret's got to catch her flight back to college. The airport is all confusing, though. Help her through the maze of the airport so she can get back in time.

Stolen Goods

The Country Club next to the Park steals stuff from the Park and turns some of the objects into toilets. Match the stolen items with their owners.

"World's Best Boss" Award

For a lot of people, summertime means an internship. Thomas the intern loves his internship at the Park, and wants to give Benson the "World's Best Boss" Award. Draw the award for him.

Dieting. It's the worst word ever for Muscle Man. He's gonna stuff his face with all his favorite foods before starting his latest diet. Use your mad drawing skills to "cook up"* his favorite foods.

*Do not actually cook these pages, because that would be bad. Just draw food that Muscle Man can eat.

College Life

Margaret is taking Eileen on a tour of her college. Draw all the sites and scenes, like the football stadium, the classrooms, the crazy campus square, and the hangout spots.

Road-Trip Planner

Summer break! The guys gotta blow this town on a road trip! Here's the checklist of everything they need for a great road trip!

_____ Snack foods
_____ Pillow
_____ Music player with headphones
_____ Camera

They also need a place to go. Draw a map of where they're going on their road trip.

Fill in the Blanks

This summer, the guys had a ton of fun when they should have been working. Help Benson write up a report about the awesome stuff the guys did!

Mordecai should've been _____ like I said, but instead he _____ with _____ and _____. I told Rigby to _____, but he decided to _____. He thought it was _____. Muscle Man and Hi-Five Ghost took off to _____. They _____ a lot of _____. I was _____ with Skips because he _____. He's a/an _____ employee.

Benson has been captured by Evil Party Guys. Draw the rest of him to free him.

Rescue Mission

Rock 'n' Ro

It's time for Mordecai and the Rigbys to go on a rock 'n' roll tour. But they've got to travel in a big tour bus. Draw the designs on the outside of the bus on this page, and then on the next page, draw the glamorous insides!

Street Performances

Performances on the street are weird, but cool. Rigby is decked out in silver like those robot guys. But there are a bunch of other street performers who are moving in on his territory. Draw 'em.

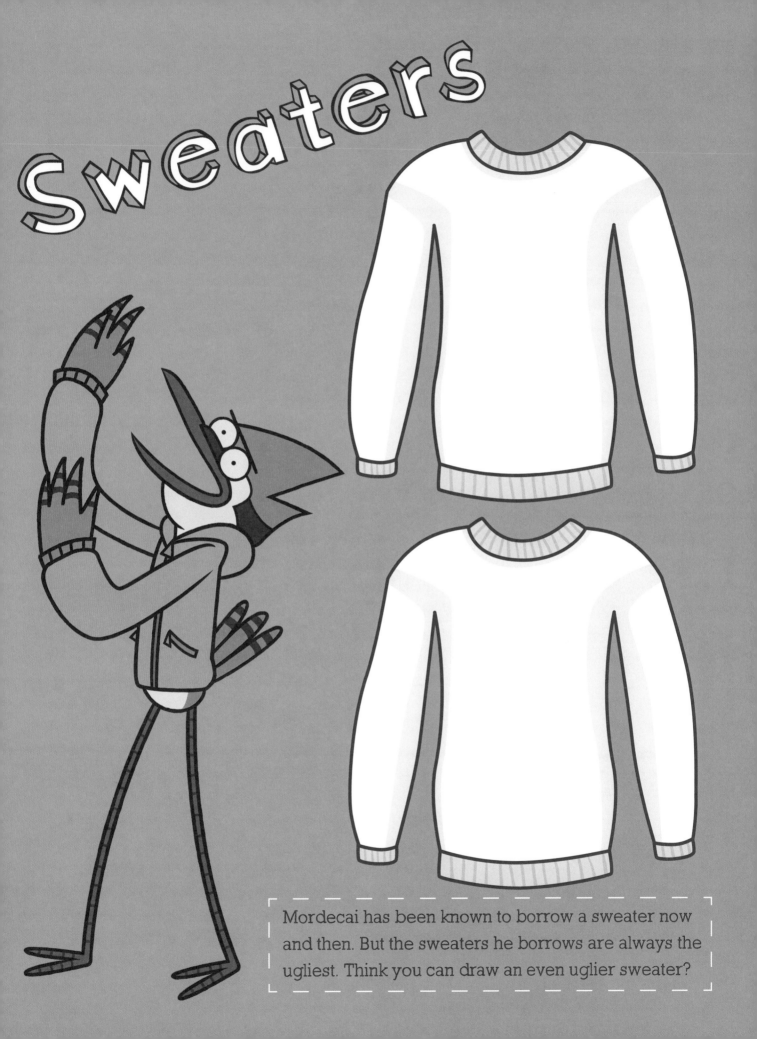

Sweaters

Mordecai has been known to borrow a sweater now and then. But the sweaters he borrows are always the ugliest. Think you can draw an even uglier sweater?

Cleaning a Messy Room

Benson told the guys to clean up their room or they'd be fired. But they can't clean it up if it's not a mess! Sketch out total pigsties in these rooms so they can clean them up—and not get fired!

Time Travel to the Past

A time-traveling tornado has sent the guys to the past! What would the Park look like in the time of the dinosaurs? Don't forget to dress the guys in caveman gear!

Time Travel to the Future

The time-traveling tornado has flown the guys forward to the future! Show us how the houses are all futuristic and stuff. So are everybody's clothes. And the cart can fly! Sketch it!

Pops loves to wear tants (table pants). What kind of weird clothes do Mordecai, Rigby, and everybody else want to wear? The crazier the designs, the better.

Tants and Other Weird Clothes

Wilderness Survival

Mordecai and Rigby got lost in the forest, and they are going to be there for a while. Using stuff from the forest, make a shelter, find some food, and hook up those guys so they survive the wilderness!

Scary Stories
(Writing and Drawing)

The guys have a bet about who can tell the scariest story at their party. On the next couple of pages, write the scariest story you can imagine, and draw some freaky illustrations that will blow the minds of your friends.

Dates

Mordecai is going to ask CJ out on a bunch of dates, but he's pulling a Mordecai and can't think of what to do. Help a brother out, and write a bunch of date ideas for them.

Stunts for Stuntmen

Muscle Man and the rest of the Park crew have trained to be stuntmen. Now it's time to perform a bunch of stunts. Draw their stunts, and make sure there are a lot of explosions, skydiving, and stuff like that.

Dodgeball

Mordecai is in a dodgeball tournament. Pummel him with dodgeballs. Draw as many dodgeballs slamming him as you can!

Soccer Celebration

The guys just won a big soccer game! They're celebrating their win with a party in the Park. Color and draw the celebrations!

Postcards from a Ghost

Hi-Five Ghost got a postcard from a lady from his past. He's sending one back to her. Write his message for him.

Sinkhole Diving

There's a big sinkhole in the middle of the Park. Lots of stuff has fallen down there. Draw the items that have fallen in: the cart, a video camera, phones, Pops's lollipops, a refrigerator, TVs, and more!

Rockin' Guitars

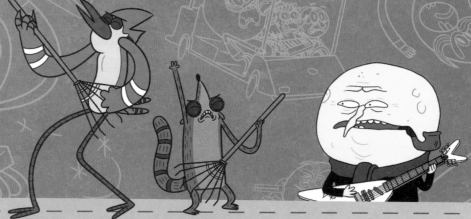

Mr. Maellard has an amazing guitar collection, and he's always on the lookout for a cooler guitar. Draw some new guitars that Mr. Maellard is gonna want so bad.

Autocorrect

Mordecai is trying to text CJ, but autocorrect keeps screwing up his message. CJ is totes confused.

 Mordecai: _____

 CJ: What? What does that even mean?

 Mordecai: _____

 CJ: You're being weird.

 Mordecai: _____

 CJ: I don't get it.

 Mordecai: Stupid autocorrect. I meant: You're awesome, and I want to hang out.

Portrait Paintings

Mordecai has to paint portraits of his friends. Help him out by sketching the portraits first.

RIGBY

CJ

EILEEN

MUSCLE MAN

SKIPS

BENSON

Cooling Down

You've been a drawing fool all summer long. I bet your experience has made you a better artist than when you started. Here's the pic of Mordecai and Rigby from the warm-up page. Draw it again, and see how much better you are this time!

The guys love playing video games. All their favorite characters are being combined into one epic game. Draw the biggest video-game battle of all time!

Include every possible game you can think of!

Answers

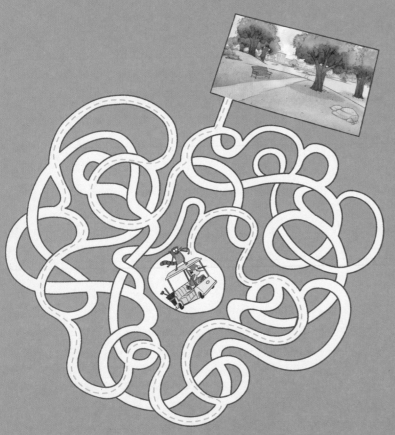

START

FINISH